Search and Find
Princesses

TOP THAT

Licensed exclusively to Top That Publishing Ltd
Tide Mill Way, Woodbridge, Suffolk, IP12 1AP, UK
www.topthatpublishing.com
Copyright © 2017 Tide Mill Media
All rights reserved
0 2 4 6 8 9 7 5 3 1
Manufactured in Zhejiang, China

The royal day begins

The princess is awake bright and early. Her bedroom is full of princess things. Can you help her to find her favorites?

Can you find?

1 kitten

2 vases of flowers

3 cake boxes

4 teddy bears

5 bottles of perfume

Can you find?

What's cooking?

Something smells good in the busy palace kitchen! Can you help the princess to spot her favorite kinds of food?

1 chicken

2 pizzas

3 cakes

4 plates of macarons

5 apple pies

Can you find?

6 pastry swirls

7 loaves of bread

8 sandwiches

9 blueberry tarts

10 strawberries

1 watch

2 vests

3 panties

4 pairs of boots

5 pink hats

What to wear?

What will the princess wear today? She has so many clothes to choose from! Help her to find these items so she can make her final selection.

Can you find?

6 purses

7 pairs of gloves

8 tiaras

9 fans

10 yellow dresses

Breakfast for a princess

The hungry princess is ready for a royal breakfast.
Can you find these items in the palace dining room?

**1 bowl
of eggs**

2 hams

**3 boxes
of cereal**

**4 plates
of cheese**

**5 cartons
of juice**

Can you find?

6 champagne
glasses

7 pots
of jelly

8 strawberry
tarts

9 gold
goblets

10 pastries

Can you find?

1 kitten

2 lollipops

3 pink flowers

4 bees

5 spiders' webs

The royal family... and friends

The princess walks through the royal portrait gallery every day. Can you find these things hidden in the room?

Can you find?

6 pale
blue hearts

7 white
mice

8 blue
birds

9 bows

10 blue
butterflies

Getting ready to ride

The princess never misses her daily ride. It's her favorite thing in the world! Can you find all the items that she needs to look after the horses?

Can you find?

1 sleeping kitten

2 brooms

3 ropes

4 silver cups

5 saddles

Can you find?

6 brushes

7 straw bales

8 red pails of water

9 rosettes

10 horseshoes

Can you find?

1 spotty butterfly

2 blue butterflies

3 lilac butterflies

4 red butterflies

5 green butterflies

Beautiful butterflies

The butterfly house is the perfect place for the princess to practice drawing. Can you find all the butterflies fluttering in the scene?

Can you find?

6 aqua butterflies

7 yellow butterflies

8 purple butterflies

9 pink butterflies

10 orange butterflies

Sewing lessons

Like all princesses, this princess has sewing lessons, but the room is a mess! Can you find the sewing items hidden in the scene and help her to clear up?

Can you find?

1 thimble display

2 sets of hat boxes

3 sewing boxes

4 pairs of scissors

5 cross-stitch pictures

Can you find?

6 jars of buttons

7 knitting needles

8 feathers

9 rolls of ribbon

10 balls of light blue yarn

Royal treasures

Sometimes, the princess sneaks into the treasury to look at the crown jewels. Can you search and find these royal treasures?

Can you find?

1 suit of armor

2 crowns

3 swords

4 scepters

5 tiaras

Can you find?

6 gold goblets

7 silver candlesticks

8 bead necklaces

9 rubies

10 gold orbs

1 dog

2 jackets

3 wigs

4 pairs of pants

5 wheels

Royal transport

This room is where the royal coach and equipment are kept. Help the princess to spot these things.

Can you find?

6 harnesses

7 hats

8 feathers

9 horse tiaras

10 bugles

Can you find?

1 sleeping gray cat

2 white mice

3 maids in gray

4 soldiers in armor

5 coachmen

"Smile, please!"

It's time for the royal family and their staff to have their photograph taken. Can you search and find these things in the busy, happy scene?

6 flower displays

7 butlers

8 candelabras

9 footmen

10 chairs

An indoor garden

The princess loves the palace garden room, full of sweet-smelling flowers. Can you find these things hidden in the pretty scene?

Can you find?

1 sleepy cat

2 ornamental trees

3 bags of soil

4 pairs of gloves

5 seed trays

Can you find?

6 small pink flowers

7 blue watering cans

8 flower baskets

9 chairs

10 bees

Fun with friends

The princess and her friends are playing in the games room.
Can you spot all these fun things to play with?

Can you find?

1 trampoline

2 black knight
chess pieces

3 cricket
bats

4 pool cues

5 skipping
ropes

Can you find?

6 rackets

7 croquet mallets

8 table tennis bats

9 tennis balls

10 shuttlecocks

1 barking dog

2 harps

3 music stands

4 electric guitars

5 guitars

Royal rehearsal

It's time to practice for the royal concert. Can you find these items hidden in the palace music room?

Can you find?

6 sousaphones

7 trumpets

8 purple recorders

9 bugles

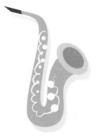

10 saxophones

Can you find?

1 chocolate cake

2 plates of macarons

3 gold teapots

4 plates of sandwiches

5 cups and saucers

Time for tea!

Princesses love afternoon tea! How many of these things can you find hidden in this sweet scene?

Can you find?

6 pink desserts

7 ice cream sundaes

8 cupcakes

9 iced buns

10 plates of grapes

Can you find?

1 ham

2 chocolate cakes

3 plates of cheese

4 roast chickens

5 green desserts

Banquet basement

The princess is in the basement, looking at the food for the royal banquet. How many of these things can you spot?

Can you find?

6 plates of sandwiches

7 loaves of bread

8 strawberry tarts

9 trays of strawberries

10 apple pies

A relaxing bubble bath

The princess is having a relaxing bubble bath before the grand ball. Can you find these things hidden in the bathroom scene?

Can you find?

1 blue bottle of shampoo

2 pink brushes

3 pink ducks

4 piles of towels

5 blue sponges

Can you find?

6 red scented oils

7 bags of cotton balls

8 heart-shaped soaps

9 green body washes

10 purple perfumes

Busy butlers

The butlers are busy polishing all the royal silver, china, and glass. How many of these things can you spot?

**1 big
serving dish**

2 teapots

3 jugs

**4 cake
stands**

**5 serving
bowls**

Can you find?

6 candelabras

7 silver ice buckets

8 round plates

9 tall glasses

10 cups and saucers

Special guests

The guests are arriving for the grand ball. Find all of these people and things at the royal reception.

1 princess in pink

2 princesses in blue

3 bowing princes

4 princesses in yellow

5 flower displays

"Dinner is served"

The table in the banqueting hall is groaning under the weight of all the food. Can you spot these tasty dishes?

Can you find?

1 dish of pears

2 green desserts

3 plates of grapes

4 hams

5 plates of sandwiches

Can you find?

6 roast chickens

7 dishes of strawberries

8 fruit towers

9 ice cream sundaes

10 pink desserts

Let's dance!

The guests are dancing and having fun. Can you find these things in the busy ballroom?

Can you find?

6 golden sofas

7 lost fans

8 chairs

9 maids

10 flower displays

1 floating princess

2 tables

3 butterflies

4 shooting stars

5 candles

An evening swim

When the party is over, the princess and her friends go swimming in the rooftop pool. What can you spot?

Can you find?

6 flower displays

7 piles of red towels

8 green rubber rings

9 beach balls

10 pretty glasses

Can you find?

1 pink broom

2 sleepy kittens

3 blue boxes of ribbons

4 pairs of shoes

5 pairs of boots

Sleepy maids

The sleepy maids are worn out! Can you find these things in their big, quiet bedroom?

Can you find?

6 dolls

7 dresses

8 teddies

9 pairs of slippers

10 caps

Royal peace and quiet

The princess loves her little turret room.
Can you find all her favorite things?

1 sleeping kitten

2 wall candles

3 slices of cake

4 bunnies

5 tiaras